NIGHTFEATHERS

by Sundaira Morninghouse
illustrations by Jody Kim

FIRST EDITION

OPEN HAND PUBLISHING INC.
Seattle, Washington

Morning Story

Last night I was sleeping
but this morning I awake
find my zebra beside me
and my fuzzy kitty Cake
I toss off the covers
and jump to the floor
cause it's morning
it's daylight
and I want to be sure
that my mom is there sleeping
and my poppa too
in their big bedroom bed
with the covers that are blue
cause the last thing I remember
was their kiss on my forehead
and their singing way of saying
"Goodnight, sleepy head"

Sun Dance

Hey there
sunbeam
how-do-you-do
that slow slow shine
from the closet to my shoes

Bright beam warm beam
on my window pane
how would you like to
play a little game of
shadow today

Hickety Pickety My Black Men

Hickety, pickety my black men
are such, such gentle men
They love me and laugh me
and tie my shoes
And squeeze me and please me
and wipe my boo hoo's

Hackelty, packelty my black women
are gracious, gracious lovely women
They walk with me
talk with me
braid my hair
and take me with them everywhere
To market, to dentist, to doctor, to store
And yes, to the playground
when their feet get sore

Hush-a-Bye Baby

Hush-a-bye baby
in the tree top
the wind blows the cradle
and my, how it rocks
birds come to whistle
stars bend to gaze
at the pretty brown baby
who spends all her days
rocking in tree tops
dancing in wind
higher and higher
she twirls and spins
an autumn leaf dancing
a chocolate-kiss star
in a sun-sweet forest
of loving arms

Rain Song

Very high in the sky
big gray clouds
floating by
plish plash
on my hat
mizzle drizzle
down and down

Feather weather
ooze our shoes
as we go splashing
two by two
drip your drops
plip your plops
tinkle sprinkle
round and round

Glitter sky
so high
pitter patter
ping and clatter
pit-a-pat-a
rat-a-tat-a
touch the ground
sing your sound

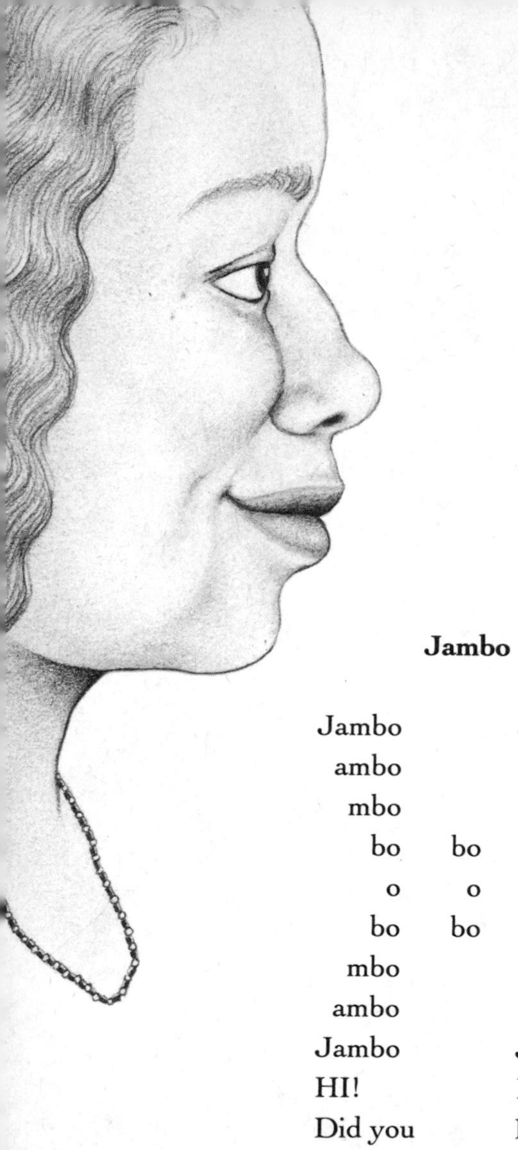

Jambo

Jambo		Jambo
ambo		ambo
mbo		mbo
bo	bo	bo
o	o	o
bo	bo	bo
mbo		mbo
ambo		ambo
Jambo		Jambo
HI!		HELLO!
Did you		Did you
did you		know
Jambo		means
hello		hello!

Outside Out

Watermelon watermelon watermelon rind
lemon lemon lemon peel
potato skin potato skin
egg shell egg shell
pea pod
peach fuzz
apple core, oops!

What Are Little Boys Made Of

What are little boys made of?
chocolate and cream
caramel and toffee
espresso espresso
and deep rich coffee

What are little girls made of?
walnut, cherry and pecan pie
mint tea mint tea
my, oh, my
swirling with honey
spiced it seems
with cinnamon, nutmeg
and laced with cream

Dogs on the Corner

Two dogs on the corner
right by the store
What are those dogs
standing there for?
What if they bite me?
What if I scream?
What if they make me
drop my ice cream?

A

All the Way Home

Rain and robots
tumble in the sun
blooming lakes
roller skates
rumble and run
Sigh sky
clear and high
don't go away
Rasheed and Zakia
hopscotch
forget-me-not
asphalt catwalk
all the way home

Roses Red

Roses red
violets blue
I wish we grew more flowers
don't you?

Once my grandma had some
they were really nice
plastic blue and red ones
that smelled outa sight
She had them on her table
right by the magazines
and each time we came to visit
they made my momma sneeze!

Mamacita

Mamacita
I love to meet'cha
coming down the street
How was work?
What a pretty skirt!
Did you buy something good to eat?

Mamacita Mamacita
can I stay outside and play?
Oh-yes! Oh-yea!
I will play
on the steps
with Elisha and Kay
And when the sun is almost down
I'll turn around
touch the ground
stamp my feet
jump across the street
and come inside for supper!

Ding Dong Bell

Ding dong bell bell
I can never tell tell
who's on the other side
of the ding dong bell bell

Is it the mailman?
Is it Jonny Wright?
Maybe it's Dracula
lurking out of sight
Maybe it's my teacher
coming to spend the night
But then, it could be T.C. Jones
coming to pick a fight

Should I open it, yes?
Should I open it, no?
Boy, it's really hard to tell
the peephole is so high
and I . . . well . . . well . . .

Tric
or

Lanterns Light Our Way

A princess in a sparkling gown
a clown whose tie tickles the ground
alligator with bright green teeth
what have you got that's good to eat?

Three bats with nightblue baskets
shriek to a skeleton "Walk faster!"
a giggling ghost is eating toast
Dracula's swinging from the lamppost
bunny hops
Wolfman cries
Cleopatra skates on by

Jack-o-lantern
pumpkin pie
owlets fly across the sky
leaves crackle
cats meow
scarecrows scare
dogs howl

Trick-or-treat
the dark is deep
the moon and stars
have gone to sleep
but lanterns light our way

Come out
come out
come out be seen
this night glows
with Halloween!

Glitterblink Twinkleshine

Glitterblink
twinkleshine
starbuds
on the skyscraper line

Cream round whipped
thin as a kiss
moon, oh, moon
halved and spooned

Stormy and rolling
leaping and folding
clouds zoom by we

Night sky watching
giggling and talking
my best mom
and
me

Besito

Buenas noches
mi corazón
the sun is gone
but your nightlight's on

Duerme duerme
mi corazón
here is a besito
for your delicious cheek

I will dream of you
you will dream of me
in our dreams together we'll sing
mi corazón
mi corazón
tú eres mi corazón

Littleboy Pete

Littleboy Pete lost his sheets
and couldn't tell where to find them
he was dreaming too
in the night deep blue
with a shiver and shake
he cried out awake
"Sheets, sheets, where are you?"

Pete woke up to find
with a shiver and sigh
the sheets crumpled at the foot of his bed
he found them indeed
curled beyond his brown knees
a-glow in the light of the moon, the moon
a-glow in the light of the room lit with moon

Pete lifted sheets to him
a moon sea flowed through him
and rocked Pete away to dream it seems
of moonbeams in starlight
of wishes and night flights
a-glow in the light of the moon, the moon
a-glow in the light of the room lit with moon

PETE

Night in the Lap of Morning

Night so smooth
night so deep
night in the lap of morning
night in the arms of another night

Sky dog black as night
come let me hold you tight

Night so smooth
night so deep
night in the lap of morning
night in the arms of another night

Moon tiger
when you leap
stars start their falling

Night so smooth
night so deep
night in the lap of morning
night in the arms of another night

African bird
fly home to me
fly across the deep blue sea

Night so smooth
night so deep
night in the lap of morning
night in the arms of another night

Caw crow
caw up a moonbow

Night so smooth
night so deep
night in the lap of morning
night in the arms of another night

Midnight caterpillar
keep crawling
birds have gone to sleep

Night so smooth
night so deep
night in the lap of morning
night in the arms of another night

If Wishes Were Midnight

If wishes were midnight
I think I would ride
right through tomorrow
and come out the other side

If wishes were moonbeams
you know what I'd do?
I'd swallow them quickly
and taste them all through

If I could say "here"
and there it would be
I'd wish for whatever
would make me happy

Nightfeathers

Gemma Nightfeather
zooms each eve
over puddle parks
on rooftops dark
with starberry trees

She slips over treetops
she tumbles on our porch
and yawns around corners
that bend around the park
turning blue and blue
until she turns quite black
and glistens up a starry show
for Zebby, me and Cat

From her wings
all these things
moonbeams
starbuds
twinkling city lights
and
shadows of shadows
with thin thin stems of light
fall onto my city
and
blow through it's streets
blow and grow
bloom and go
sun sun
sunflowering
into the bright blue
tall wall
we call
sky